excerpts from the book i'll never write

NADIA STARBINSKI

ISBN: 9781549893339
Imprint: Independently published

To all whom are lost

ACKNOWLEDGMENTS

This is for my best friend's mother who said she couldn't wait to see my name in print. This is for the boy who loved me through it all and pushed me to become everything I am today. This is for my English teacher in high school who said I had no talent. This is for the friends who never allowed me to give up on myself. This is for my coworker who started every shift with an encouraging word. This is for my followers who begged for content. Lastly, this is for myself. Who's doubting of my integrity and refusal to live to my potential went on for way too long.

i. love

LONG DISTANCE

The thing no one tells you about falling in love is the loneliness of missing them. Falling in love with someone from across two bridges, a tunnel and state lines. There's cravings that will never be fulfilled, a never ending lust for an interaction that is otherwise deemed impossible.

When it's 3am and I've collapsed into my pillows from the overwhelming emptiness that hovers over me at the early hours of the morning, there is no driving over for a hug. There is no midnight fast food runs or early morning diner dates. There is no "come outside" or "open the door."

And on nights like tonight when I crave your arms more than the oxygen in my lungs, the extra distance between our hearts stings a little more than usual.

...AND THEN I FELL IN LOVE WITH YOU

He was shy and mysterious; mysterious but in a good way. Like receiving a box of chocolates from a secret admirer and trying to match up the individual flavors to those tiny pictures in the lid.

He had this quirky awkwardness to him that made him all the more beautiful and mesmerizing.

He made days seem longer when I was caught in his rays.

I was lost in the crystalline caves of his sea-glass eyes wandering into a day dream and trailing after sleepy sentences as they burst into February air and fade into whispering under the blueness of the night.

I find myself watching as the sky bleeds over the trees into the early morning, breathing my own clouds of cold atmosphere as my chameleon colors melt into the frozen ground.

Like a mirror falling beneath my feet.

I've spent all hours of the night contemplating the words to say to you, but no combination of twenty-six different letters could ever accurately capture even a sliver of what this feeling is.

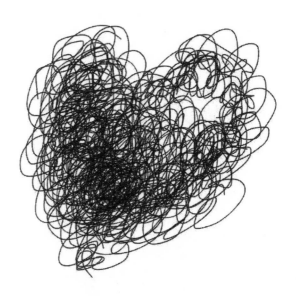

SERENDIPITY

_____

"Needed Me" by Rihanna had become my summertime theme song. I had convinced myself I was fine on my own. I was tired of my heart being dragged along with broken promises and temporary "I love yous". I was tired of trying to break my wall down, just to build it up again. It became a heartbreaking cycle I didn't want to be on anymore.

So I stopped looking.

I stopped looking for the guy who was going to want me for me; who made me feel comfortable and not ridiculous for being passionate about something; someone who didn't just want to be tangled in the sheets with me but have something of substance.

I craved a forever not a just for now. I don't want to play games and feel anxious when I haven't heard from him in a while. I don't want to wake up every morning second-guessing myself or wonder what I had done to justify the distance between us.

Then you came along and I was thrown off guard.

I've always preached about everything happening for a reason and the best things happening when you least expect them, but when I first met you during freshman year of college, I thought and felt absolutely nothing. We spoke here and there and we formed a very casual friendship. As the semester progressed and we found we had more classes together, those short hellos in passing turned into full-blown conversations about sports, our friends and hangover stories- to say the least; we were bros.

Slowly but surely those conversations in class expanded to conversations via text message or snapchat and we became closer than just school friends. The boundaries never overstepped the strictly platonic friendship we had besides the occasional "are we ever going to hang out outside of the classroom?"

Then over *two years* later, after maintaining that friendship, you decided to finally take me up on the offer. We met up in the parking garage outside a movie theater in-between both our towns and after the initial awkward hugs and "how've you beens," we were back to our old joking around selves. The vibe was effortless and the chemistry was undeniable.

The first thing I thought when I realized I was falling in love with you was, *Shit.* It happened right before my eyes: the guy sitting across the table in my freshman English class, who I used to text about the really awkward dates I went on and give advice about his then-girlfriend, transformed into the person I wanted to be kissing at the end of the night. It was an electric feeling — like I got zapped — and suddenly I realized everything was about to change in a big way.

The thing about dating your best friend is it's almost like living in a real life movie. It's more than just having a boyfriend; the romantic relationship develops after you already have a strong friendship together. Best friends know each other inside out; there's no shame in dressing like a slob or staying in instead of going out. He's closer to you than your closest girl friend, because you not only have a romantic chemistry together, but there aren't any formalities or restrictions from being your true weird self.

When you date your best friend, it's more than just a physical and emotional relationship. You deeply connect on a personal and mental level as well. To say the least, I never understood the concept of dating a close friend until I met you.

You're intoxicating. You set my soul on fire. Being in love with you is something I can't even put into words. It's like time just doesn't exist with you. In the blink of an eye it's 4pm and my body is still tangled up under the sheets with yours. Being in love with you feels like a baby's laughter. The kind that you feel throughout your whole body- where you can't muster up any noise, you just shake with complete joy (even though you think it's annoying).

I never thought I could feel this sense of security with a significant other. The thought of being in your presence just drives me wild, I know I'll never have to worry as long as you're by my side. Being in love with you feels like I have known you since the beginning of time. Like my heart couldn't find its rhythm until it beat next to yours. We often sit staring into one another's eyes, no words need to be spoken. I can feel my heart beat faster, and a smile softly tugs at the corners of your mouth.

Your scent makes my knees weak, and you're always there to steady me with your strong hands. You have a sense of humor (no matter how many times I'll deny it). Your laughter is booming, and it's contagious. You accidentally shove me too hard and grin down at me like it was the most adorable thing you'd ever seen, despite the original wave of concern and guilt. You make me smile every day.

You're selfless. You drop me off when it's late so you can assure I get home safely. You'd take the shirt right off of your back if you sense that I'm even a little bit cold. You show me every day that you love me. You open every door for me, you carry my things for me. You remember every stupid little detail. You surprise me with pizza and kisses.

You are just unlike any other man I have ever met. You're open with me about what is on your mind. Whenever there is a conflict between us, you are patient with me and understanding. You always put me first. You remember what's important, and what's not. You always tell me you never want to lose me, and I promise I will never let you go.

Being in love with you feels like I am actually me. Like I spent so long going through life blindfolded and now I can finally see. The way I feel about you, I cannot put into words. Your endless patience and persistence allowed me to open my eyes and see what was in front of me all along. I know the bond we share is very rare these days but I can't think of anyone else I would want to be with at 2:30 in the morning when I can't sleep and I crave your arms around me.

And I wasn't expecting it. I wasn't expecting you.

Being in love with you feels like falling into your bed after a long day at work. Like this is where I am supposed to be. I just look at you and I am home.

———————————————————

OUTSIDE THE BOX

Let's run to the end of the city where the lights shine the brightest. I promise not to leave you behind, if you promise that our time spent will be the time in which we find love at its finest.

A love that is patient and kind and undying; a love that leads us to create our own personal Zion.

And once created, a place that will call for us until we arrive, and only then will we be at peace; sitting at the edge of the world with the skyline behind us.

It is here where I'll ask you to be mine, the only label needed in this world dull of self-proclaimed designers.

Liars who create boxes with uncomfortable liners and force us into them without reminders

That we can choose not to live in any one box or be any one socially constructed item.

A place where it will be only you and me, from sunrise to sunset, and the world will be ours with no complications or compromises.

_____

THESE HANDS

I dream that one day you will wander into a book shop and thumb through the pages of titles you didn't know existed. You will be entranced by a description of his hands on the steering wheel, and you will think *this can't be* as you purchase the book.

You will take it home and toss it on the counter, where it will stay as you take a shower and cook your dinner. It will feel as if it's staring at you while you eat, and after dinner you will sit down to read it; hoping that hearing its voice will shut it up.

Your hands will be shaking as you read well into the night.

When you have devoured the final page you will lower the book to the floor and sit with your head in your hands, the same hands that once rested on that steering wheel, and you will know that some things hit too hard to be forgotten.

———————————————

IT

_____

I can't claim to know much about love.
I know it's a sensation though. Like
being on the edge of a precipice or
perched at the top of a peak, frightfully
aware that when you decide to dive
into its valley, butterfly wings are the
only things to keep you afloat.

But somehow it's enough.

Somehow featherweight seems safe.
Somehow *fragile* would manage to be
sufficient in cushioning your fall. And
often we do. Fall, that is. And that's not
the part that hurts. It's the reeling
realization that there's no one to help
you work your way back up.

That mountaintop is too far off, and not
even a flock of doves could take you
above, to where love loiters. I know its
disappointments as well. Because
you've spent so long culturing pearls in

oysters of her eyes, only to find them devoid of treasure. That displeasure lies in her depths, and you're nothing but the shipwreck beached on banks of "no thanks."

I know its directions too. It's flow of away, like the sway of the receding sea. I also know that love's a one way street. That you give, it takes and while you say break for it, *it* will stop to whisper in your ear or wipe away your tears. No, it'll merely continue pulling its strings like a puppeteer, until you're withered and weary.

So I know a little. Maybe the problem is that *it* doesn't know me?

———————————————

ii. loss

EXCERPTS FROM THE BOOK I'LL NEVER WRITE

—————————————————————

I have fallen out of love with my art. Virginia Woolf once said, "I am overwhelmed with things I ought to have written about and never found the proper words."

That's where I'm at.

As a writer, my world is vibrant. My thoughts are consuming and every experience is followed by a philosophical analysis which often leads to the scribbling of excerpts from the book I'll never write.

I haven't written in a while and I'm starting to fear I've forgotten how. I feel this overwhelming darkness begin to devour me and I'm scared my skeletons are beginning to peak their heads out of my closet.

I am sad.

Not in this beautiful way that everyone romanticized.

I am anxious.

Not in this aesthetic where claiming to have mental illness is worth bragging about.

I am lost.

In every definition of the word.

I am suffocating, yet I am the one holding the bag over my head.

_____

LOST

———————————————————

I don't really know how to write anymore. I mean, really write; from the heart or soul or wherever the hell all the painful stuff comes from.

I want to write about a beautiful kind of love, the kind that people spend their whole lives dreaming up. But when I try to form the words from my mind, they don't conjugate well and I end with a jumbled mess.

And no one dreams of a love like that; a jumbled mess.

Somewhere between the words on my tongue and the veins in my soul, I lose my words; my expression.

I lose myself.

_____

SELF HARM

I burned my tongue when I kissed you and I guess that should've been the first clue that this would go up in flames

but I kissed you anyway and now my whole body is on fire and you said you would put me out

and insanity, by definition, is doing the same thing over and over again but expecting different results each time

if this is so then Jesus God I should have been committed a long time ago.

Because I can't see how any sane person can continuously reach for the scolding pan expecting the sting to eventually subside

and as much as I wish the pain would disappear, I'm beginning to believe I never did.

"I love you," I whispered into the midnight air.

"I just need a drink," she sobbed.

I reached down and grabbed the aged wine bottle from her fragile fingertips. I looked into her eyes, gray with age and exhaustion, and she looked into mine with a certain sadness that broke my heart.

I put the wine on the table and held her in my arms the way she held me when I was a child. Like a thief in the midnight air, an angel gained her wings.

"So this is what it feels like to grow up?" I thought to myself, "To have every sense of innocence stripped from you in a matter of minutes?"

I was forced to grow up that night as I held my grandmother's heavy heart in my arms.

"I told my sister not to leave me and she did."

———————————————————

POISON

Some nights I think about dying and some nights I think about living until I break.

And I didn't know that you could cry so hard that your heart stops bleeding and still wake up the next morning, until I met you.

I know that kissing you will probably kill me, bury bullets beneath my skin and spit poison into my veins but I know I'll kiss you anyway.

And sometimes shaky knees and feeling like you're going to throw up, and staying up so late you get sick is love and not pain.

But sometimes the teeth you feel when you're kissing and the way the red of the flowers he brought you matches the red in the sink and the way the butterflies in your stomach make you feel like dying is pain and not love.

Either way I never know when to say goodbye so maybe you should just stay one more night....but Jesus, I'd swallow poison if it tasted like you.

———————————————

They meet a total of two times.

Once, when her heart is sixteen and sprightly, drowned in sunbeams and smiles and all too ready to fall too deeply in love. Again, when her heart is tired and broken, exhausted by days, months, years too plentiful in which she let her legs collapse and let the people around her continuously push her down.

First, he sweeps her away with a single curve of his lips, lets crescent-shaped eyes sway her into reaching out and when she does, he takes her hand and whispers promises of never letting go. He tangles fingertips into her hair and presses clandestine kisses against the crown of her head. There is something about the way he lets flowers bloom against the canvas of her skin that makes her forget the way those very same roots begin to creep up her throat and constrict her breathing.

He is beautiful-maybe not aesthetically-intoxicating, a star so small in the nebula that there isn't anything she can do but notice him. It is his touch she falls in love with, his crooked smile, and the way his laugh reverberates off the walls of the room, of her chest, of her heart. It is the way his voice fills her lungs with joy and her heart with some indescribable warmth that she falls in love with.

It is the idea of hands fitting together perfectly and legs tangling beneath sheets in perfect harmony that she is in love with.

She is not in love with him.

She was never in love with him, so she doesn't know why she clings,

because he leaves.

His footsteps resonate in her mind like thunder and her mind is flooded in that final instant by everything that changed- everything she willingly distorted for the sake of her own delusions of serenity.

When he leaves her pillows stop smelling like flowers and sunrise, but like cigarette smoke and the ashes of something she can't quite identify.

Second, she lets herself waste away and waits patiently for the flowers pressed against her skin to disintegrate and die like the rest of her being. She waits for the roots to cripple and crumble; she waits every day, waiting until she can take that deep breath she's always wanted to take.

But secretly, she picks at those flowers and lets sunrise soak her pillows. She lets dusk act as her blanket and dances her own fingertips against the top of her head when she's stumbled out of bed, pretending that they aren't her own, but his.

She pretends that things haven't changed too much. She's still the same minus the sporadic moments where she holds her own breath because she can't tell if dusk is suffocating her or if those roots of those flowers fading from her clavicle are growing with each tear she sheds over an empty space in her life.

She pretends the world around her is still spinning, that the stars in the sky still twinkle and that the birds in the morning still chirp as loudly as possible.

But what she can't find herself feigning is her own happiness, because when the sun bids adieu and she's sitting on the edge of her bed, brown orbs fixated on what lies behind the dirty panes of her balcony window, all she does is squint because she thinks in that leftover orange hue she might find the imprint of his smile.

She thinks that in the ebony blanket of the sky, she'll find that star in that nebula tiny and insignificant but still peeking through that curtain of dusk.

They met a total of two times.

The first time he captures her heart and lets it break.

The second time, she picks at the shattered pieces of what remains and lets her mind paint a picture, an idea that he is still there.

Her fingers spread apart and she closes one eye and uses the other to see through the gaps, making sure to be careful not to miss that tiny star in that giant nebula.

I MISS YOU

_____

It's 2am and my arms searched for yours from under the sheets.

What a horrible way to wake up.

_____

SUICIDE

There are plenty of ways to kill
yourself.

Stick a gun to the back of your throat,
fall asleep in the garage with the car
on, jump into a river and let the rock in
your chest where your heart used to be
drag you to the bottom, smoke too
many cigarettes, bleed yourself dry.

I think the most effective way is kissing
someone who's name you will never be
able to say without shaking.

WHISKEY

Lately I've been holding bottles instead of you because it's 4am and I'm grasping for you but my hands only find cold sheets and my bed doesn't smell like your cologne, just the whiskey I spilled on my pillow two nights ago.

---

iii. acceptance

GOODBYE

I never let myself go anywhere with the fantasy of me and you. I outright rejected the idea before you could reject me, but I couldn't stay away.

I never let myself touch you because I was afraid once I began I would never be able to let go. I turned when you grazed my hand because my heart sped at such a rate that I was sure you would hear it, or if not by my instantly flushed face. But you made a comment instead about me loosening up, patted me on the shoulder and walked away.

We hugged goodbye, and I tucked my face into your shoulder. I was drunk, so I let myself fall into you completely.

You took me in, absorbed me, and when it was over, the smell of your aftershave lingered for far too long.

CHROMA

Silence is a painful thing. Like a secret.

"Shhh," she said, "close your eyes; don't say a word." And you listen because that's all you know. In those few moments in between when your weary eyelids counterbalance your unfledged skin and a sweet slumber begins to dwindle, there are those thoughts that race through your frivolous mind.

It is in that silence where you can hear everything. Her mold in the sheets casts a hue of purples and greens on the shades that ignite the room and as her breathing becomes more acute you realize the things around you are beginning to fade into a bleak nothingness, yet your eyes are closed.

It will not be until the chroma of daylight begins to bleed through the curtains that once depicted the elegant illustration of a beauty you did not know could harmonize within your vacant walls, here is when you will unravel your eyes from your deep gaze only to question your dreams and realities.

Because in that silence one can no longer tell whom he is destined to be. In that silence she is nothing but a vague figure of your subconscious.

A figure of a thousand faces and you are forced to put the puzzle pieces together. It is here in the silence where you will spend the rest of your existence deciphering between fact and fiction, and in all of this...your eyes will be closed.

SELFISH

Sometimes there are people who come into your life and leave a permanent mark. They paint your soul different colors and change the way you see the world.

When they leave, you realize that somewhere along the way you lost yourself. You don't even know who you are anymore because they made you into something completely different.

I don't miss you.
I miss myself.

DEMONS

"Look back," he said, "It's all so different from over here.

> "I don't want to look back. I don't ever want to go back there. It was so dark and cold over there."

"You can't forget my dear; it's an awful thing to…forget."

> "But I want to forget, why would I want to remember so much pain?"

"You must learn from it," he whispered," It is an important part of you."

> "That wasn't a part of me. Those were the demons inside of me."

"You musn't let the demons win my child."

> "How do you kill the demons inside without killing yourself?"

"Look back," he insisted, "It was so beautiful over there."

GONE

_____

I wish I had said…
Differently.
At least showed some emotion,
Or asked you what was wrong.

I wish I had said…
Okay, instead of being so stubborn.
I always have to get my way, you know
that.

Yes, I wish I had said…
You were right.
You were always right.

And now I can't. Oh, how
I wish I had said…
You mean the world to me.
You always knew me best.
I love you with everything in me,

Yes, that is what I wish
I had said, but,
I didn't, and I couldn't.

All I said was...
Nothing. I gave blank stares.
And now, you're gone.

———————————————

WORDS

Words.

You are falling asleep on the floor beside a notebook and your favorite pencil because your life is nothing but a meaningless throng of words.

But you can't fall in love with words, you know. I've seen it happen. I've felt winds of words that lift bumps off my skin as I loan my breath in exchange for nostalgia.

They grow wings in my heart and flutter down into my stomach, keeping me awake at night, shivering.

THAT'S ALL THAT MATTERS

_____

Thoughts of you tend to sneak up on me. They never come at night, in the safety of the dark. Memories are not forged beneath my eyelids waiting for me to close them.

You come in the swipe of a metro card- you promised the night you made me jump that you would pay my ticket if we got caught, but we didn't so you bought me a pretzel for bravery instead.

You're in the sneezes of strangers, because they did it three times too. You are the crooked smile of the guy at Barnes & Nobel who laughed at a stupid joke of mine.

Or the stranger on the corner of Spring
and Broadway who stayed on the curb
rather than edging forward with me.
Or the one in Starbucks hunched over
two different notebooks; the student
running with the aged NorthFace
backpack.

But you're not here anymore.

And that's all that really matters.

—————————————————

PURPOSE

_____

I think there are people that you are supposed to let into your life, and I think that by design they are meant to leave and you are never supposed to speak again.

And these people rip your heart out and feed it to the sharks. They dare you to break the rules and sneak in through the windows. They sit on shingles and whisper impossible promises into your ear.

If you are standing up, they turn you upside down. They have you running toward midnight with little more than an eyebrow raised. You'll remember the oddest things about them- like the way they say "hilarious" or the TV shows you watched at 3am on a couch that smelled like salt water and bad decisions.

Then one day, you'll wake up to find they are gone and you will recognize the finality of that word.

Gone.

Because you will know that it is physically impossible for something so random and so perfect to happen twice. Whenever the streets flood with rain, you will think of them.

They will be the dark shadow in your dreams, the black figure that you can never catch up to no matter how quickly you try to run.

_____

iv. growth

You're always going to shrug your shoulder and tell everyone you haven't changed that much.

You say this until someone catches you off guard at 2:30am and says, "Tell me about yourself."

And you reply with, "Like what?"

And they say, "Everything."

It is when you're explaining your life from when your mother neglected you, to the one night stand you regret and you are brought back to the present and truly realize...you are not the same.
Then you sit back, take a deep breath, exhale and say,

"Thank God."

GROWN

_____

If you can open your eyes
And get lost in the beauty of the sky,
If you can't tell the difference between
When the earth and heavens collide,
If you have seen a shooting star and
hoped
With all your soul that your wish may
come true,
If you have the faith to pursue your
happiness
And accept the truth hidden in the lies,
If you can hear the deafening silence,
Sit in a room full of shadows
And feel only the presence of yourself,
If you can hear their screams without
seeing their mouths move,
And close your eyes – be real with the
horrors of today.
Then you, have grown.

_____

5AM

_____

You say "it's 5 o'clock somewhere" as
you drown your insides with vodka

but what happens when it's 5 o'clock
somewhere

and the sun begins to peak it's head
through the curtains of the sky

and you're drunk off the idea that the
premature sunlight will wash your sins
away.

You can't water the flowers in your
soul with the finest pinot noir

and you can't set alarms to remind
yourself to turn over and wrap your
arms around the sun.

This too shall pass and the aching you feel for the kiss you never won will eventually subside.

You will learn how to fall asleep without him next to you

and you will learn to love yourself far more than he's ever claimed to love you.

―――――――――――――――――――――

WOLF IN SHEEP'S CLOTHING

I am a firm believer in never holding grudges. I refuse to bring my hurt from past relationships into my current endeavors. That being said, I **should** have trust issues. I **should** be this stereotypical bitter female who's sworn off boys and goes to bar crawls on Valentine's Day, but I'm not. I am quite the opposite.

I love to love. This has been brought to my attention in the past as some tragic flaw of mine. The idea of being a hopeless romantic in a society built on the foundation of a hook-up culture is somehow unwanted; too passionate, too intimidating, if you will. That being said, when I met this "Mr. Perfect" who shared similar values on relationships and pretty much checked off everything on my list; well...I just knew.

Sometimes you know. You look at this beautifully crafted silhouette of a person and you ask yourself how you got so lucky. Maybe it was that smile, the way his skin formed crescents around his seductively pale lips when he grinned so absentmindedly. Or maybe it was those eyes. Those caramel coffee bean colored eyes that looked like nothing less than sunshine gleaming through whiskey, those eyes that looked at me and sent a jolt through every fiber of my being.

I knew with him. I knew he'd be bad for me. Nobody that perfect is placed in your life so precisely, so blissfully, with the best of intentions. It didn't help when he knew all the things to say to keep me swooning 24/7 yet consistently kept me on my toes. You hate to be this negative person but in a weirdly confusing way, it really does become too good to be true.

I knew he'd tear my heart right out of my chest and crush it into a fine dust in his hands. I knew he'd be the most perfect heartbreaker I'd ever have the privilege of loving. Somewhere deep down I knew he'd be the worst choice I'd ever make. But I went on choosing him anyway, day in and day out through every battle through every test he'd put me through; I chose him. Then there comes the point in a relationship where you can't stop ignoring the signs. The insecurities that build up, the doubts, the uncertainty;

everything you ignored because you were so fascinated by what was in front of you with a big red bow and a tag that read, "All Yours."

But that's the problem- I hold on to the memories instead of people. I love so much that I continue to fall in love with a person that doesn't even exist anymore. There's a certain thrill to it, the danger of falling in love with the idea of somebody rather than who they actually are.

I don't know what it was for sure; I have no idea what it was that made me love someone so selfish and inconsistent. All that I know is I loved him, my God, I loved him with all that I had, and that love broke me from the inside out until I had nothing left to offer.

Moral of the story, there are plenty of wolves out there, and you won't be able to spot them so easily at first. You're going to find someone who passes so flawlessly on every relationship criteria you have. He's going to butter you up and send you in this fantastic bliss. But beware, because that same person is going to be willing to shove love so far down your throat that you won't be able to get the bitter taste out of your mouth for weeks.

Love yourself enough to know when to walk away. Don't invest so much time and effort into someone who will be able to wake up one morning and no longer see the stars in your eyes. The best love is not manipulative, it is not inconsistent, and it is not selfish. The best love is confident in himself, he knows who he is and what he wants and will turn those stars into constellations.

"Love is patient, love is kind. It does not envy, it does not boast, it is not proud. It does not dishonor others, it is not self-seeking, it is not easily angered, it keeps no record of wrongs. Love does not delight in evil but rejoices with the truth. It always protects, always trusts, always hopes, always perseveres. Love never fails." 1 Corinthians 13:4-8

_____

RECYCLED MEMORIES

———————————————————————

I threw away the last boy I was in love with today. I stopped holding onto words and pages and I threw them away.

Well I recycled them, had to be sixty pages of memories spread over three years.

I met him when I was sixteen. I haven't spoken to him in a year. I hardly think of him now, but I had these pages; proof that once someone at least believed that they loved me. That's what was hard to get ride of.

Without them, I have no proof, and my mind only shelters contorted memories and the silent demon giggling in the corner of my brain tells me that no one will ever love me like that again.

That is why the world will let me chase my ambition, because it knows success doesn't equate happiness.

———————————————————————

CONFIDENCE

Reading is something I've always struggled with, reading aloud that is, to an audience, budding ears eager to hear me lift the words from the pages that their eyes are desperate to read through, waiting for my voice to walk their eyes long the lines that tells a beautiful story. But I would always be crippled by nerves that told me I wasn't good enough.

The thing is, I've always lacked the confidence to read aloud, my voice trembles with fear and cowers under the strains of expectation, I always feared that my voice could not read with conviction, that my voice was too inferior to carry the words that would resonate deep within the ears of those willing to listen, that I'd fail to do justice to the characters so meticulously crafted by the author. In my eyes, the beauty of good literature deserved the beauty of a good voice to read it to others. That was until I met you.

You forced me to read to you, every night. You said you couldn't sleep without it and I wasn't about to be the one that kept you up all night. So I read to you, and sure enough I struggled at first. My voice not much more than a whisper, carrying words with no conviction, telling stories that lost their substance when my voice carried them.

In time, however I realized that above all you were just eager to listen. You appreciated that I was reading to you, and you never questioned or challenged my ability to do so, and I guess that was an amazing gift in itself.

Because it let me row in confidence, it allowed me to read to a sea of people with poise and strength.

I could send chills down your spine when I read to you. I could make you quiver and shake. I could seduce you, just by reading to you. And I guess I really have to thank you, because you gave me that ability to read aloud. Without your help, my voice could barely squeak let alone roar as it does now.

The thing is though, I wish just once you had read to me. Just to know what it is like to fall asleep to the sound of your voice.

_____

_____

I am not here to tell you it's going to be okay because you already know that. Anyone can tell you that.

I am not here to stitch up your wounds.

I am not a nurse or a doctor. I don't know how to fix you and I wouldn't want to try. I am here to tell you that it's time to heal. It's time to let go of the years you've lost to your misery. The years you've spent falling in love with your sadness and the way your bones look when there's nothing but skin over them.

Stop planning out your funeral and stop writing your suicide note. Save your energy for the love letters you will have to write one day. Save your good stationary. Stop staring at your veins like they will bleed answers.

Some days, you will still feel the hollow

sort of heaviness like your bones are made of iron pipes. All you need to hear is that it is okay to be sad for no reason, a billion reasons, or for one small reason.

Some days your lungs will bleed and the fresh air is made of salt. Some days your skins will be a wound and the world is nothing but acid. On these days, you need to know that it is okay to cry.

Some days you will feel naked and vulnerable like when sadness left, he took your whole closet with him. I am writing this because none of us can be saved. None of us can be fixed, because there's nothing that needs fixing. You are you. Do not listen to the boy who tells you that you are broken because he hasn't bothered looking into a mirror.

Some days, loud noises will still feel like needles on your skin. People will raise their voices and they will ask why you are scared of them. Some days you will still cringe when men touch you. There will be days when you will go the beach wishing the sea were made of alcohol so that you can stop dreaming in black and white. You will wonder why they've put you on so many drugs and you will ask yourself why you can't function on any less.

On days like this, there are only a couple things you must remember: you've been through worse before. You are limitless. The things you are capable of are infinite. There is someone waiting to tell you how proud they are of you for making it this far. I am writing this to tell you that it's time to let go of your walls, your ceiling, your floor and grab onto the sky.

———————————————————

AUTHOR'S NOTES

A dear friend once told me that I had the power to turn just about anything I touched into something beautiful. Given the proper care and the nurture of that as a mother's gentle touch, anything could be struck easily as gold. It had never occurred to me that this talent that I possessed could have easily carried me through life. I was too blind to see that with a little caressing of the mind and the willingness, which I once held as a young child, would prepare me for this great success later on in life.

I was a washed up composer, a one hit wonder with the potential of a prodigy. Only one little detail hadn't been accounted for – the fact that I *wasn't* a prodigy. All my life I had been told by teachers how amazing I was, how they had never seen an eight year old convey such emotion through pen and paper before. Test after standardized test my writing scored would soar through the roof. While children my age were worrying about getting caught under the bed sheets late at night with a flashlight and a comic book, I was writing.

The later I stayed up, the more I wrote, the better I became. It was this weird form of intellectual child-born heroine addiction that formed in my tiny second grade brain. I was hooked.

I would go through about five 99 cent notebooks a week and each day with a new poem, anecdote, or my personal favorite – adventure stories. I would place my main character, Penny Pigtail, in situations where she would always prevail. No matter what her struggle was, gum in her braids, imperfect grades at school, she would come out victorious or a crowned hero.

In every sort of way, Penny is much like me; the hero to my own story.

Made in the USA
San Bernardino, CA
06 September 2018